Landforms

# DESERTS

by Laura Perdew

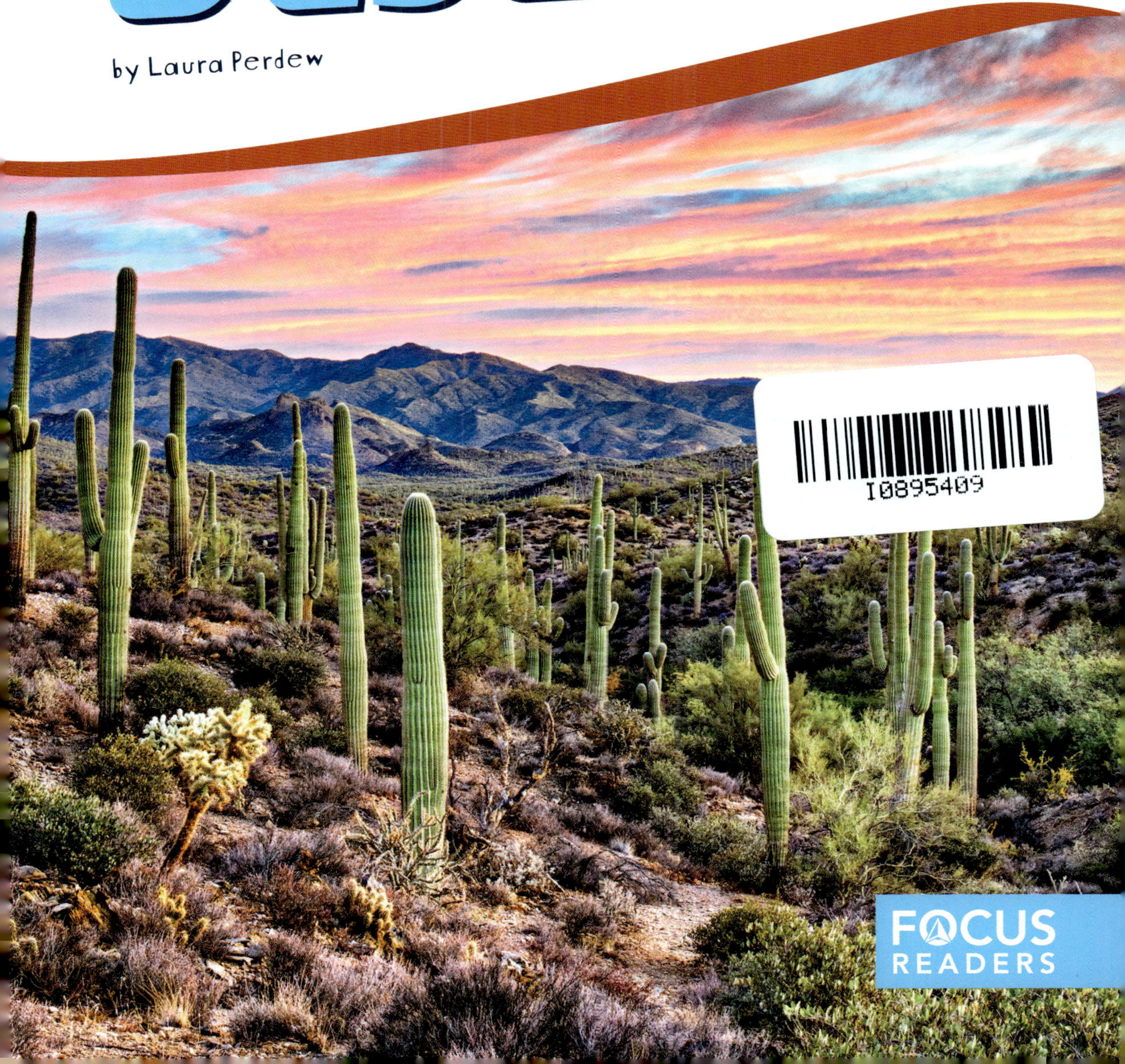



FOCUS READERS

FOCUS READERS

www.focusreaders.com



Focus Readers is distributed by North Star Editions:
sales@northstareditions.com | 888-417-0195

Produced for Focus Readers by Red Line Editorial.

Photographs ©: Anton Foltin/Shutterstock Images, cover, 1; Breck P. Kent/Shutterstock Images, 4–5; Bill45/Shutterstock Images, 7; Adisa/Shutterstock Images, 8–9, 29; Efimova Anna/ Shutterstock Images, 11; Anton Petrus/Shutterstock Images, 12; Filipe Frazao/Shutterstock Images, 14–15; Rhys_Palazzolo/iStockphoto, 16–17; Denis Burdin/ Shutterstock Images, 18; Everett Historical/Shutterstock Images, 21; sevenke/Shutterstock Images, 22–23; Nicholas Taffs/Shutterstock Images, 25; Martha Marks/Shutterstock Images, 26

**ISBN**
978-1-63517-892-0 (hardcover)
978-1-63517-993-4 (paperback)
978-1-64185-196-1 (ebook pdf)
978-1-64185-095-7 (hosted ebook)

**Library of Congress Control Number: 2018931689**

Printed in the United States of America
Mankato, MN
May, 2018

## About the Author

Laura Perdew is an author, writing consultant, and former middle school teacher. She writes fiction and nonfiction for children, including numerous titles for the education market. She is also the author of *Kids on the Move! Colorado*, a guide to traveling through Colorado with children. Laura lives and plays in Boulder, Colorado.

# TABLE OF CONTENTS

CHAPTER 1

# WELCOME TO THE DESERT

Waves of heat rise from the dry ground. The sun above is scorching. Cacti stand tall and quiet. Everything is still. As dusk falls, life begins to stir. The desert awakens.

**The Sonoran Desert in Arizona has many saguaro cacti.**

Deserts are very dry places. All deserts receive less than 10 inches (25 cm) of rain per year. Even when rain does fall, the water **evaporates** quickly. Some deserts are hot and sandy. Others are very cold. Some deserts even have mountains.

**FUN FACT**

**Death Valley is in the Mojave Desert. The highest temperature on Earth was recorded there. It was 134.1 degrees Fahrenheit (56.7°C).**

The Racetrack Playa in Death Valley is known for the lines formed by stones pushed by the wind.

Deserts may look barren. But most of them are full of life. They are home to many types of plants and animals. Every **continent** on Earth has at least one desert.

CHAPTER 2

# HOW DESERTS FORM

All deserts are **arid**. This is because the wind does not bring much **moisture** to them. But there are several types of deserts.

The equator is an imaginary line that goes around Earth's middle.

The Sahara is a huge subtropical desert in Africa. Very little moisture falls from the sky there.

Near this area, the air is hot. It has a lot of moisture, too. This air rises. Clouds form. Then the moisture falls back to the ground as rain. Cool air is left behind. This cool air moves away from the equator. When that happens, the air warms quickly. As a result, few clouds can form. And without clouds, rain cannot fall. This creates a subtropical desert.

Coastal deserts form because of cold ocean **currents**. These currents cool the air. This process creates

Fog hangs over the Namib Desert. It is a coastal desert in Africa.

fog near the shore. But very little rain can form. The air may seem damp, but rain does not fall. The ground stays dry.

Other deserts have summers that are long and dry. The winters are cool, with little rain or snow.

The Gobi Desert is in the rain shadow of the Himalaya mountains.

Some of these deserts are formed because of mountains. The mountains force the wind to go up. Clouds form, and rain falls on the mountains. But the air that flows beyond the mountains is dry. This creates a rain shadow desert.

Other deserts are in the middle of continents. Rain falls to the ground before the clouds get to the middle of the continent. These interior deserts stay dry.

Where **polar** deserts form, the air is often cold and dry. That means few clouds can form. So, these areas get very little rain or snow.

**FUN FACT**

**Earth's largest desert is in Antarctica. It is a polar desert.**

# THE ATACAMA DESERT

The Atacama Desert is in Chile. It is one of the driest places on Earth. Most of this desert gets less than 0.2 inches (0.5 cm) of rain per year. Some parts get no rain at all.

The Atacama is more than 600 miles (1,000 km) long. It sits on raised, flat land between two mountain ranges. Because it is high up, the Atacama is cold.

Only small numbers of lizards, insects, mice, birds, and foxes live in the Atacama. But hundreds of plant species survive there.

**The Atacama Desert includes salt flats that are home to flamingos.**

CHAPTER 3

# DESERTS CHANGE

The **climate** on Earth is always changing. This causes deserts to change. Over time, some deserts become larger. Deserts can grow because of farming, water use, or forests being destroyed.

The Great Victoria Desert is Australia's largest desert.

The Sahara is almost as large as the United States.

Many deserts today didn't used to be deserts at all. The Sahara is a good example. Long ago, this area was very green. It was full of lakes and grasslands. But approximately 5,000 years ago, the area's climate changed. The Sahara is now hot and dry. It is the largest hot desert in the world.

Humans can also cause deserts to grow. This can happen when people drain water in an area. Humans need water to survive. However, when they remove too much water from an area, the land in that area dries up. Plants die. The ground can **erode**.

Deserts can also form when people use land carelessly. For example, having too many farm animals can create deserts. The animals eat too many plants. Without the plants, the soil erodes more easily. Soil and plants usually hold moisture. But without them,

## FUN FACT

In the 1930s, huge dust storms on the Great Plains of the United States turned many farms into deserts. This area became known as the Dust Bowl.

Much of the Great Plains region of the United States became a desert in the 1930s.

an area dries out. Humans work to prevent this process.

CHAPTER 4

# LIFE IN THE DESERT

Plants, animals, and people have **adapted** to live in desert climates. Some desert plants, such as cacti, absorb and store water. This allows them to live without rain. Other plants have a waxy coating.

A cactus's spines prevent animals from eating it.

This coating keeps water from evaporating. Some plants have deep roots. They reach water that is far underground. Other desert plants grow far apart. Because of this, they do not compete for water.

Animals have adapted to the desert, too. They can survive with

## FUN FACT

**After a rare rainstorm in the Atacama Desert, more than 200 types of flowers bloom. They cover the desert with color.**

The kangaroo rat doesn't drink any water at all. It gets all the water it needs from the food it eats.

very little water. Many desert animals get water from the food they eat. In hot deserts, most animals come out only at night.

A black-tailed jackrabbit's large ears can send out extra heat from its body.

They use shade or underground holes to avoid the sun. Jackrabbits have large ears that help keep them cool.

Nearly one billion people live in deserts. They have found ways to collect and store water. Sometimes the water is pumped from deep underground. Other times it is brought in by pipes. People who live in the desert might wear clothing that keeps them cool. Homes in the desert are also designed to stay cool on the inside.

**FUN FACT**

**In some deserts, people travel on camels. These animals can go for months without drinking water.**

## FOCUS ON
# DESERTS

*Write your answers on a separate piece of paper.*

1. Write a letter to a friend explaining the main ideas of Chapter 2.
2. Which type of desert would you like to visit? Why?
3. What do all deserts have in common?
   - **A.** They are hot.
   - **B.** They are dry.
   - **C.** They are sandy.
4. Why do animals in hot deserts come out only at night?
   - **A.** More plants are available for them to eat.
   - **B.** Rain is more likely to fall during the night.
   - **C.** Temperatures are not as hot after the sun goes down.

5. What does **barren** mean in this book?

*Deserts may look* ***barren****. But most of them are full of life.*

- A. empty
- B. noisy
- C. strange

6. What does **scorching** mean in this book?

*Waves of heat rise from the dry ground. The sun above is* ***scorching****.*

- A. very small
- B. very hot
- C. very loud

*Answer key on page 32.*

# GLOSSARY

**adapted**
Changed over time to deal with a certain situation.

**arid**
Very dry as a result of getting little rain.

**climate**
The average weather conditions of a particular place or region.

**continent**
One of the seven large pieces of land on Earth.

**currents**
Water movements that go in a certain direction.

**erode**
To wear away slowly over time.

**evaporates**
Changes from liquid to gas.

**moisture**
Wetness.

**polar**
Having to do with areas near the North Pole or South Pole.

# TO LEARN MORE

## BOOKS

Cole, Tayler. *Cacti Barely Need Water!* New York: Gareth Stevens, 2017.

Fleisher, Paul. *Desert Food Webs in Action.* Minneapolis: Lerner Publications, 2014.

Gagne, Tammy. *Desert Ecosystems*. Minneapolis: Abdo Publishing, 2016.

## NOTE TO EDUCATORS

Visit **www.focusreaders.com** to find lesson plans, activities, links, and other resources related to this title.

# INDEX



**Answer Key: 1.** Answers will vary; **2.** Answers will vary; **3.** B; **4.** C; **5.** A; **6.** B